Suniti Namjoshi was born in India in 1941 where she worked as an officer in the Indian Administrative Service. Subsequently she taught at the University of Toronto for many years. Her poems, fables and satires have been published and widely read in North America, India and Britain. She now lives and writes with Gillian Hanscombe in a small village in East Devon, England.

Other books by Suniti Namjoshi

Verse

Poems
More Poems
Cyclone in Pakistan
The Jackass and the Lady
The Authentic Lie
From the Bedside Book of Nightmares
Flesh and Paper (with Gillian Hanscombe)

Verse and Fables

The Blue Donkey Fables
Because of India

Fiction

Feminist Fables
Aditi and the One-Eyed Monkey (children's)
The Conversations of Cow
The Mothers of Maya Diip

Translation

Poems of Govindagraj (with Sarojini Namjoshi)

St Suniti and the Dragon

Suniti Namjoshi

Spinifex Press Pty Ltd,
504 Queensberry Street,
North Melbourne, Vic. 3051
Australia

First published by Spinifex Press, 1993

Typeset in Times by Claire Warren, Melbourne
Made and printed in Australia by Australian Print Group
Cover design by Liz Nicholson, Design BITE

National Library of Australia
Cataloguing-in-Publication entry:

CIP
Namjoshi, Suniti, 1941–   .
    St Suniti and the dragon.

ISBN 1 875559 18 3.

1. Fables, English. I. Title. II. Title: Saint Suniti and the dragon.

823.914

"Justice!" cried the Sparrow,
Armed with bow and arrow.

For Gill

Acknowledgements

Some of this work has appeared previously in the following journals and anthologies: *Bazaar, Canadian Literature, Manushi, Tessera, Frictions: Stories by Women, Someday My Prince Will Not Come, The Man Who Loved Presents,* and *The Pied Piper.*

CONTENTS

Part One
St Suniti and the Dragon

Part Two
The Solidarity Fables

Part One

St Suniti and the Dragon

I

The Gilded Lilies Began
to Burn

(i)

You are my goddess, Suniti said
to the round stone, all belly and no bone.
No, you, you are my goddess, Suniti said
to the white bone, all elegance, finely honed.
Oh you, and you, and you are my goddess, Suniti said
to the women she met, of whom one or two acquiesced,
and one just smiled and shook her head.
And later, when Suniti regarded the bone with no belly,
and the stone with no bone, and all the walking,
waking women she had met, she said,
"What could I have done instead?"

(ii)

That you should laugh your foolish heads off
in the brilliant sunshine and die without
a scream makes me want to weep, Suniti
informed the pansies, then the irises,
then the poppies, then the roses, who barely
heard, aware as they were of the summer's breath,
craving the recurrent tremor of tendrils.

(iii)

In the afternoon sun the gilded lilies
                    began to burn. "Death awaits us.
Death shall amaze, and Death without effort
                    shall end our days."
"But you burn," said Suniti. "You have,
                    it would seem,
a comment to make." "We burn," said the lilies,
"in a golden blaze; but a quick white light
                    shall end our days."
"And then?" asked Suniti.
                    "Charred lilies. No more days."

II

Failed Prayers

(i)

If I could pluck out the eye of malice,
              bury it deep, let it lie;
if freed of malice, I could breathe freely
              (let earth resolve the luckless lie);
if I could watch a tree sprouting,
              barren and beautiful,
and stand there casually while its golden apples
              poisoned the air;
then I could say, "Ah, Malice worked.
              Malice did it,"
as I walked away, breathe a sigh.

(ii) She Plucked Iridescence . . .

"This stone?" asked the angel. "Are you able
to rejoice in it?"
I stared at the stone. "Is it precious?"
But the angel missed
my cautious hint. "Well, then this feather?"
She plucked iridescence
from the casual air. Of course it was rare,
of course beautiful,
but would anyone else believe in it?
"In what?" asked the angel.
"In feathers falling from angels' wings."
The angel laughed.
"How shall I prove it?"
"What?" I ventured.
And the angel smiled – a bright, beatific,
bountiful smile,
"That your happiness matters, and that Angels can
prove very kind."
Well, I could have asked for a few thousand pounds
or a modern miracle;
but that's not how it works.
I bowed my head. "Thanks," I mumbled.
"It's not very often
that one meets an angel. . ."
but she looked crestfallen;
so I picked up the feather, and this time
I smiled.

(iii)

Birds flickered in the branches.
Hoar frost covered the ground.
Suniti brought out breadcrumbs.
It made her feel profound.
"A heart heavy with woe,"
she suddenly informed a sparrow,
"would make you fall, you know."
She imagined the fallen sparrow,
was aware of an intricate grief;
when the dead bird rose and flew,
and sang for disbelief.

III

"'Tis the Eye of Childhood . . ."

(i) Sir Suniti and the Fearful Dragon

She mocks herself.
　　She has done her best to cast out pride.
But this gorgeous fear
　　　　　　　(which makes *her* gorgeous)
– was this the Fear she sought to hide?

(ii) She Imagines Herself Facing Death

If I could face Death unafraid,
then surely I would be a Conquering Maid?

(iii)

Afterwards she set out to find her fear. It was not a white hart, luring her with beauty, but transparent and fluid. And it did not lead her into a forest among benign trees, but onto rock-hard pavements, crowded with people. And there it took fright. It leaped into her body. Liquid panic slithered through her, invaded the most remote and tiny capillaries. Her eyes turned to glass; she knew that if anyone touched her, their fingers would freeze, or she would freeze. She felt alert and a little sick. But the fear was turning into crystals now. If it crystallized, she would die of it. The fear must be made to mix with her blood, take colour from it.

She made herself breathe. She allowed the fear to flow freely. When at last she was convinced she would continue to live, she looked about her. Fear was home safe. Now who should she hunt? How kill?

(iv)

"Perhaps fear is unkillable," she announced ponderously. "Perhaps it's a mythical and immortal beast." Perhaps – and with this thought her heart rose – perhaps this quest is a failed quest, and it is not my duty, much less my aim, to attempt to kill it. She glanced at the dragon lying at her feet. And then, in a flash, saw herself standing there, at the foot of the dragon, puzzled and puny. Perhaps fear is only a large animal . . . Even so, it did not follow that she had to kill it. On the contrary. She stroked the dragon. Nothing happened. Though large and shapeless, it wasn't slimy. Perhaps it was dead? But it was patently absurd that she, as a saint, or even as a woman, should have to climb up its flanks and stick a flag in its body. She would not do it. She could see it was breathing. But perhaps it was dying? Was it her task to end its misery? Would it not be better to allow it to live, to fulfil, so to speak, its own destiny? She patted its sides, the dragon groaned. "Help me," it begged. "Please help me." She watched aghast. Who was she to help a heaving dragon? She distanced herself, but the dragon had whelped. She found herself wriggling in a welter of babies.

(v)

Though birds and beasts sing
    and Suniti claimed she witnessed
            everything,
the canny and clever
        could not discover
what the dragon said
        when nobody else
           was listening.
Suniti said, "He heaved and groaned,
        sighed and moaned. . ."
Suniti said, "The dragon skin
        collapsed from within.
The dragon died. In his progeny
          he was glorified."
"And," she said,
        "the dragon screamed,
a fearful, final, fluting scream.
        I dreamed he screamed.
Then he died."
        But they said
           Suniti lied.

(vi)

Suniti shrugged. She had done her best to give evidence, even to the point of open confession; she had not been believed. It happened sometimes. They had said the dragon survived. She had said the dragon died. There was no contradiction. She would bury the truth in a new jingle. Let them dig for it.

No one sober in spring. Pluck each dragon seedling.
Gather them up in a green salad-bowl.
They squeak and they shriek, they pule and they howl;
But pat them and pet them, feed them on cake.
Fool the little darlings. Make no mistake.
When the dragons are grown they'll quickly devour
The life in your veins, the bliss in your bower.
Then stroke them and strike them, kiss them Good Bye.
Dragons must sleep if dragons won't die.

With that Suniti staggered to her feet, loaded a syringe and anaesthetized the dragon babies one by one. The effect was instantaneous. They froze without protest and turned into pebbles. It was as though she had managed to freeze-dry them. They could not sprout without careful watering. Concentrating hard she slit her left breast and tucked them away in a waterproof bag.

Then she examined her conscience. The deed was done. But had it been well done? A full grown dragon was in constant danger from passing saints and brave civilians. She had ensured the safety of saints and dragons, also of civilians. A medal was in order. She glanced at the sky, but the tree overhead proffered only apples. She munched an apple. It occurred to her that police and politicians might outrank saints under certain conditions.

IV

The Trials of the Saint

It so happened that as St Suniti was walking down the street, absorbed in thoughts concerning the complications of a saintly life, she was suddenly confronted by Grendel and his Mama. The old hag leered at the saint. "Hey Sunny!" she called. "We're going to have to eat you, you know. It's not for myself, you understand, but Sonny Boy here is starving to death and I've got to feed him." Suniti glanced at Grendel, a long adolescent with hungry eyes; she looked away quickly. It was a difficult situation: could she talk her way out?

"Please Madam," she began tentatively, "as a fellow woman you are surely unwilling to fatten your son by victimizing me?"

"Willing or unwilling, don't really matter," the Mama replied. "He's got to be fed and that's about it." Then she looked cunning, and in a fair imitation of Suniti's voice, added slyly, "But surely, Sunny, as a fellow woman you ought to be willing to aid and abet?"

Suniti was stumped only for a moment. "I am," she replied. "Come with me and I'll help you to find him something to eat."

Now as the saint and the mother, with Grendel in tow, stalked the streets, the women ran away or hid in their houses, as did most of the men, though there were one or two who were either too drunk or too brave to take any notice. "Eat them?" Suniti suggested. Mama glanced at Grendel inquiringly, but Grendel just stood there and looked obstinate. His mouth quivered. It looked as though he was getting ready to howl.

"Poor darling," his dam explained. "He has a strong preference for female flesh and he's getting hungry." She looked at Suniti appraisingly. "You had better find him something quickly," she said.

By now they had reached the outskirts of the town and the saint was getting desperate. Only a few days ago she had resolved to take a vow of abstaining from meat; but surely in an exceptional situation an exception might be made. 'Besides, I needn't partake,' she told herself.

"Wait here," she told the two monsters. She left them huddled by the side of the road and set off rapidly across the fields. Almost immediately she saw a rabbit; but by the time she had bent down to pick up a stone, the rabbit had vanished. She took the precaution of picking up a number of stones, but saw no more rabbits. Time was running out, and she hurled a stone at a passing cat. She chased it briefly. At the second try she hit her target, but she could not find the corpse.

She was cross with herself, 'I should have cajoled it.' Still, there was no time to waste worrying about what she ought or ought not to have done, or about whether or not she had actually killed the cat. In front of her was a field of cows. Her eyes brightened. A cow would do! She was sure that a cow couldn't run very fast. Indeed, some of the cows were approaching her. But the stones in her pocket would just bounce harmlessly off a cow's back. She looked about for a large rock with which she might be able to brain a cow. She had heard that if you hit cattle in exactly the right spot, they fell down dead. But she couldn't see any rocks, and in any case she didn't know the right spot. Perhaps if she had a sharp stone, she could slit the cow's throat and take the blood to Grendel – as appeasement so to speak? Then bring Ma and Grendel back and let them finish the job?

Just as she began to sort through the stones, she heard a crashing in the hedgerow. Time had run out. Grendel and his Mama had come to attack. The saint summoned all her fortitude. "Hello," she called out cheerfully. "I was just coming to get you two. Look, here's a whole herd of cows that you can have." For some reason her words weren't producing the right effect. Grendel and his Mama were glaring at her.

"I – I was just about to slit the throat of that cow over there and bring you her blood. The thing is," she attempted a quick, embarrassed smile, "I haven't a container. . ."

Her voice trailed away. Grendel's Mama took a step forward. "My son," roared Mama, "only eats human flesh."

St Suniti gave up at this point. She waited for Grendel to tear at her body. But Grendel was sobbing in the background somewhere. In between the sobs she heard him say, "She's not a proper woman. I'm hungry, Mama. I need a woman's flesh." For a moment Suniti couldn't understand what was happening. She saw Mama turn, and in the dim light she saw her begin to suckle Grendel. Aware at last that the monster had rejected her, Suniti walked away and left them to it. She wasn't quite sure what she felt, though of one thing she was certain: her sainthood was in shreds.

V

P.C. from Paradise

A few days later Suniti embarrassed all her friends. "Do you think," she asked, "that I ought to give up my aspirations to be a saint?"

"Yes," said one. "No," said another. "Depends," said a third. "Depends on what being a saint means. Why don't you ask a proper saint?"

Reluctant to admit that she didn't know any saints and unsure whether she would recognize one, Suniti paused to think for a moment.

"But how are saints to be snared?" she murmured. "What is their habitat? What the conditions? The conventions and customs? I mean where do saints live?" She looked inquiringly at the group of friends.

"In paradise," said one.

"In solitude," said another.

"In obscurity," said a third.

"In India," said a fourth, who was inclined to be facetious. Suniti ignored her.

"Do you mean," she asked incredulously, "that saints as a rule remain unknown?"

"Yes!" they all said. The unanimity of the response made Suniti despair. Her friends felt sorry. "Listen," they told her. "You worry too much. Take a holiday. It will all seem different when you get back."

"All right," Suniti agreed, turning away.

"And send us a postcard," they shouted after her.

"Okay." She set about doing what she'd been told to do. These were the postcards Suniti sent.

(i) P.C. from Paradise

Here where the climate is warm, the grass
luxurious, and every delicacy so lightly
pressed that my only vexation
                              – if it is one –
is how to refuse with appropriate grace;
oh here in this agreed and agreeable paradise
the blessings are so lavish

                              that it's probably true
I am a saint.
(Thus Suniti, languid and lazy,
and for once superbly pleased with herself.)

(ii) Glass Bottle P.C.

Adrift on the back of the deep, blue sea
– no one along for company –
Suniti asks if possibly
she's at last living blamelessly.

(iii) P.C. Sent Aloft by Carrier Pigeon

Then happiness
> rolled over her like green waves.
>> The water perhaps, or the warmth
>>> of the sun? She felt loved.

She scrambled ashore,
> forgot happiness, just wanted to know:
>> if a passing saint had happened to see her,
>>> would the saint have somehow approved?

When Suniti returned, her friends asked if she'd met any saints.

Suniti shook her head.

"Well, don't give up," they advised briskly. "Saints do exist. There have been reports and repercussions. Echoes through history. There are problems, of course. Saint look-alikes, camouflaged saints, and the well-known fact that the saintly life tends to be brief. But look around you. Just keep looking."

"Right," said Suniti and looked.

VI

The Line Up

(i)

In the line up of saints, bitter blue eyes,
    the fury craven, the bitterness burning:
"And what is your claim?"
                        "Pain," he cries.
"Violent and visible. My evident. . .
                              suffering."
Suniti looks, observes with some wonder
              the grace of his flanks,
the bloodied lips. A beautiful saint.
                    An artist made him.

(ii) To the Second Candidate

And what do you offer?

                Thirty years work.

No time off.

                A bludgeoned brain.

                        A battered body.

A pensioner saint?

                Does she count?

So out of date?

                Out of work.

                        Out of service.

(iii)

But the third candidate had an inward gaze.
She made quite plain her utter indifference
to being seen or seeing. Not a word
was vouchsafed. "Saint & Martyr"
blazed from her brow, etched in acid
of her own making.

               Suniti sighed – perhaps
out of pity – and almost offered a covering.

(iv)

At last one night a vision was vouchsafed. A saint
appeared – well documented, doing her job – exactly as
though on a television screen. What might have been
tedious – domestic chores, endless cleaning – the eye of
the camera made luminous, and the scale altered everything. She fed the hungry, clothed the poor, and she
swooped down upon battlefields. At least, once, when
the supplies gave out, she snatched a swab of sky from
the heavens and tended bleeding limbs. Suniti watched,
from a proper distance, grateful and glad that someone
was taking charge of things. She knew she was having
an extraordinary dream. It did not wake her, but all the
next day she carried with her a distinct sense of
relieved suffering. She felt she must make a poem of it.

A saint is a clod, a robot.

A saint is what

I clearly am not.

In exasperation she crumpled up the piece of paper. She
badly needed a different dream.

(v) "Star Trek"

Everything luminous –
                    a saintly world.
Even the flowers
                    beamed in unison
at the walking, talking
                    saintly beings.
Suniti eavesdropped,
                    tried,
for some reason
                    to remain unseen.
They spoke? – of pleasure.
                    Suniti squirmed,
seizing her chance,
                    she slipped back quick
to the waiting ship.
                    Then safe yet again,
off she flew
                    in the familiar search
                    for a less alien scene.

(vi)

One morning Suniti woke up with what she decided was a revelation. Trees are saints. They clothe the poor, they feed the hungry. They are not carnivorous. They live off dirt. But it's equally clear that they have aspirations, that they reach upwards and long for light. Furthermore, trees have a certain inarguable beauty.

She paused for a second to check the logic. No, her arguments were sound. They slotted in. She felt impelled to tell someone. Perhaps her neighbour, an avid gardener? She dashed outside to impart her findings, "Trees are saintly!"

"Why?" asked her neighbour.

Suniti explained.

"What about shrubs?"

Suniti stared. She wasn't sure where all this would lead, but the shrub in front of her wasn't snarling or growling or in any way doing anything obnoxious. "Them too," she replied briskly.

"Smaller plants? Poppies and pansies?"

"Lesser saints?" Suniti ventured. She knew she was getting out of her depth.

But her neighbour was relentless. "What about buttercups, dandelions and daisies?"

By now Suniti regretted she had said anything. "Fallen saints?" she faltered feebly.

Her neighbour laughed. "Why?" she queried.

Suniti gave up. "Well, perhaps you're right. Perhaps trees are not saints. Perhaps trees are merely an evolved species." She didn't quite know what to say.

"Oh, trees are all right," her neighbour responded. "They scrabble and clutch like anybody else." She lowered her voice, "The thing is, trees are discreet."

"What about saints?"

The neighbour shrugged. "Don't know about them." She looked at Suniti curiously. "I thought saints were generally human beings?"

"Oh. Oh yes, of course, you're right. Thanks," said Suniti and scurried inside.

She looked in the mirror.

Beauty had no human face.

And the tears she shed

were so much brine.

VII

Back in the Woods, Evolving Further

i) Back in the Woods

Seeing Suniti get more and more depressed, a well-meaning friend said to her, "Being a saint isn't very different from being a poet or a dentist. In order to practise, you have, in fact, to set up as a saint. Let the hungry and angry, the needy and seedy, come to you. Let the baffled sit at your beautiful feet."

"That's cheating!" protested Suniti. She was genuinely shocked. "If all I'm doing is staring into space, then what do the hungry and angry, the sullen and solemn, get out of it?"

"A concrete vision of the saintly life."

"What if the saint herself isn't having any visions?"

"Don't tell them," her friend advised.

Disenchanted and disgruntled, Suniti stalked off and flung herself on a nearby tree stump. She stared into space. Soon a woman came along whose son had been hanged for murder recently. She threw herself at Suniti's feet.

"Comfort me," she pleaded with the saint. "Say some words of comfort, please."

Suniti's face remained expressionless, but an imperceptible nod was accorded her client. It was enough for the poor woman.

"My baby is in heaven."

"Yes."

"He is singing in heaven with the sweet-eyed cherubim."

"Yes. Young-eyed."

"The murderers of my baby will be justly punished."

"Yes."

"I and my baby will be reunited in heaven."

"Yes."

"And the heavenly angels will shed their blessings."

"Yes."

"Oh thank you," cried the woman and went on her way.

The well-meaning friend, who had overheard this, now approached Suniti. "How do you feel?"

"Terrible," growled Suniti.

"That's good," replied the friend. "It shows you were trying. But practice makes perfect." She patted the saint. "Soon you'll be doing it beautifully."

(ii) Evolving Further

The following day, a fellow expatriate took Suniti aside, "If your quest is to succeed, you really ought to look into your own origins. In the East, as you know, saints write poems. . ."

Suniti was interested.

"The poems of saints are addressed to a divinity, to Krishna, for example . . ."

Suniti drew back.

"Consider the works of Sant Eknath, Sant Tukaram or Sant Mira Bai. . ."

Suniti considered. "They were great poets," she murmured at last. A thought struck her. "Are poets, by definition, always saintly?"

The expatriate Hindu stared at Suniti. Then she hunted through her mind for everything she knew about the lives of poets. Sant Kalidas? It sounded all right. But Sant Shakespeare? Shakespeare had probably not been an Indian, and she was reasonably sure that even if a church had existed, Kalidas had not been canonized. "It's not that simple," she cautioned Suniti.

But Suniti by now was bent on exploring all her possibilities. "I feel I have a better chance of being a good poet than of being of a good person," she announced earnestly. "If I concentrate on the former, do you think – "

"You'll eventually become Sant Suniti?" Her friend laughed. "You might," she told her. "In another life."

Suniti's face fell.

"Or even in this one," she added kindly.

But Suniti still looked very dejected.

"Now what's the matter?"

"Well, but whenever that happens, whether in this life or in the next, I've just realized – I won't be me!" The embryonic saint glared at her friend and sank back to dwell dolefully on the utter injustice of both luck and logic.

Manuscript broken off.

VIII

War Diary

(i) 17 Jan. 1991

For the first time in my life
            I would like to believe
that Evil is substantial;
      so that then one can clout
evil on the snout
          and fight an uncivil war.

S observes from a distance too close for comfort.

(ii) 18 Jan. 1991

They bombed Israel.

Television indicated that some? many? Muslim hearts even in Britain were gladdened by this. How is that possible? What has made this process possible?

They bombed the sands where the Republican Guard might have been hidden. How many Iraqi soldiers dead?

I notice that 'they' means the Iraqis in one instance and the Allies in another. Am I dissociating myself? I cannot, can I? As an inadequate member of an inadequate species with an inadequate response.

(iii) 19 Jan. 1991

They bombed Israel again.

I feel a little ashamed of "St Suniti and the Dragon" – all
that posturing and posing, however ironized. The moral
dilemmas are carefully planned, carefully constructed
to make them a little clearer. In the manuscript the
pictures on TV are playfully conflated with a dream,
and the dream with imaginary fields of battle.

But these are not imaginary battlefields. Real beds
with real blankets are waiting to be filled. (They
showed them on TV). And sisterly saints – not to be
mocked for they have never set themselves up – are
making preparations and waiting in readiness to do
their job.

(iv) 20 Jan. 1991

And the soldiers, the young men and the young women? They are not posing either. Even if they wanted to, they haven't the time. They haven't claimed that they're St George.

Perhaps only the poets are jobless, I mean jobless even at their self-appointed task.

(v) 23 Jan. 1991

Today at noon, with the sun shining, with buds beginning to sprout on trees, today in this pleasant and pastoral landscape, for the first time in my life, I am able to make the devil seem real. I do not know what the Christians mean, and perhaps I'm committing heresy. But this devil. Let him be male. Or female. Or androgynous. Let his skin be oily and tough – like a bat's. Let him have a snout – like some misshapen animal's. (No real animal ever looked like that.) Let him have a tail and horns – I don't mind. Let him have bad manners, vulgarity, an unappetizing aspect – I don't mind that either. But when this devil and I present ourselves to each other, this much is clear: though I cannot quite bring myself to fall upon his neck and greet him as a long lost friend – he is not a long lost friend, I did not know him before – it is nonetheless true that the cordiality in my voice is not fake and the relief I feel is genuine. The devil is not exactly my friend, and not exactly a blood relative; but there is a sense of kinship. The devil is both me and the other, both familiar and alien. The devil is human and inhuman. That is why I feel a sense of relief. It is necessary to have a devil in order to fight a war. The devil is on my side, but that means that at least the responsibility is shared. And the devil does not fight God – whoever that is. God has nothing to do with this. The devil and the human beings on my side fight the human beings, probably plus another devil (it is better if that is indubitably so), on the other side. Then we can have an epic war. We can have heroic devils. We can be demi-devils ourselves. And while all this goes on something inside me weeps and is crushed. Who? I am a creature. The devil is a creature. The creature weeps? *It weeps because it does not want to commit evil.*

I never actually said so, but what I felt was a kind of blank disbelief when I read long ago that Virginia Woolf used to go into the most profound depressions because of the war. And I once said – stupid of me – that to commit suicide at 52 didn't make sense, but now I'm almost 50. But that's a different matter. And E.P. – I wrote a dissertation on The Metaphysics of the Cantos. There was a chapter in it on Good and Evil, and I discussed what the critics had to say about E.P. not being able to come to terms with evil, about his not having any real understanding of it. They said that it just made him lose his temper and say it was something trivial like usury. And I defended E.P. as best I could because I too wanted to believe? or believed? – is it the same thing? – in the ideal, wanted to know and feel that it was achievable, that it was inherent in the ordinary world. I think I've lost touch with that earlier self, but I understand now that *E.P. had lived through 2 world wars*. As a poet, and particularly as a poet who said that politics was the domain of poetry, he had to face the fact of war. There's a bit in "Mauberly" – "for an old bitch gone in the teeth" etc. Tone? Angry. As a poet – i.e. as someone essential to society, not a luxury – he had to say something about the fact of war. Broadcasts on Radio Rome. Inadequate and unacceptable. But other poets? When they say "War Poets" they mean people who fought in the wars. So then if these poets write about the "pity of war" or the uselessness of it, it's acceptable. But what about the people who lived through a world war, but didn't fight in it, what did they say? Different for men? Different for women? In this war women are fighting.

I am a 50-year-old woman. I am supposed to be a poet. What am I doing?

IX

"... Fears a Painted Devil"

(i)

Having agreed to the existence of devils at last, it did not take Suniti long to meet her in person. (What is the relationship between devils and dragons?) The meeting occurred in a patch of daylight. Suniti had emerged from her shell for a while and was walking in the garden. She was smiling at herself, and at the trees, for having mistaken them for saintly beings. As she patted a tree trunk, she saw that entwined around a bough, a few feet above her head, was a jewelled serpent. Suniti jumped back violently. Familiar fear coursed through her. The serpent was slithering towards her now. Suniti picked up a twig in self-defence, and realizing that it was useless, threw it at the serpent. The serpent dodged. Then suddenly Suniti drew herself up, took a deep breath and overcame her fear. With immense cunning, she ran into the house and came back quickly with a saucer of milk. This she placed at the foot of the tree and, with a wide sweeping gesture, indicated to the serpent it was meant for her. The serpent hesitated, then came closer.

"Sister," cajoled cunning Suniti, "be my friend. I acknowledge you now. Live with me secretly. Bite my enemies. Teach me your skills. And for all the evil that we do, take your half-share. Or, indeed" – this with an attempt at witty generosity – "my share as well."

But the jewelled serpent said nothing at all. She drank up the milk. Suniti waited. Now she would speak. But the serpent slipped away without a word. It was clear that she had understood the meaning of the twig, and that she had understood the purpose of the milk. It was also clear that she had completely ignored Suniti's speech.

Suniti stood there, trying not to learn what silence might mean.

(ii)

Once she had reconciled herself to the view that a garden snake, however beautiful, was not evil, Suniti decided to set about the matter in a more businesslike way. She would put an ad in the paper.

> "Elderly gentlewoman seeks to make
> a bargain with the devil."

But as soon as she had written it out, she knew it wouldn't do. She would get frivolous phone calls from people who claimed that they were the devil, and weren't at all. . . They would inflict accounts of their devilry on her. It would be tedious. And even suppose that a genuine devil appeared among the callers, how would she know that this was indeed a real devil? In what way was a devil distinctive? Should she just choose the person she found most obnoxious and call him the devil? But then how could she possibly get on with him? Shouldn't she and the devil have something in common? And suppose the devil said, "Sorry, you're not a magnificent enough ally for me to want to bother with. You haven't done anything really horrible or, for that matter, anything splendid." Then what could she say? "That's just it," she could say. "You should deal with me just because I am so very typical."

For a moment, seeing herself as Humanity's Rep. in conference with the Devil made her feel grand. But then she felt confused again. She couldn't remember why she had wanted to invoke the devil. Then she remembered. She wanted the devil to share the blame. The blame for what? She didn't want to be too specific about it. Even the "News", which was supposed to be factual, wasn't doing that. Still, if she wanted to deal with the devil, she'd have to be clear. She would say to the devil, "Please, I want you to share the blame for the human condition." But then what would the devil say? What could she offer? Herself? "I am in league with the devil." She tried saying that. It was unpleasant. It was not only unpleasant, it was silly and pretentious. It was as silly as saying, "I am in league with the gods." In league against whom?

But if she dispensed with the devils and with the gods, then what was left? The human condition. But even if she agreed that she wasn't a tree or a stone or a snake in the garden, that she was human, what was she supposed to do? She had tried being good, and that was too hard. Trying to be evil seemed equally difficult. And she knew that it wasn't very different for anyone else. If she asked a passerby, "I say, do you want to commit evil?" she was morally certain that the answer would be 'no'.

So then? Perhaps it was all a colossal illusion? Illusory bodies were dying like flies on illusory battlefields? And Gloucester was saying that the gods were wanton? And Arjuna was being told to kill his cousins in a wholesale slaughter? All these worlds in a poet's head – one blow of an illusory? axe would crack the macrocosm.

(iii)

Because the world seemed flat and fallen
she conjured the creatures she had invented:
the one-eyed monkeys, the shape-changing donkeys,
and birds of divers sorts who hitherto
had flown at fancy's behest. "Wherein lies
wisdom?" she asked each of them. "In playing,"
laughed one. "In silence," said another. "In
purposefully striving," offered a third.
And seeing she was vexed, they went away again.
"Am I a bird, a beast, a donkey?" she asked
the thin air. In the real atmosphere, no
bombs fell, plants still grew, and the planetary
soil was solid underfoot. "Cause for comfort?"
a voice suggested. Who said that? Dragon
or demon? Could she tell the difference? She
stood there thinking loudly and boldly, un-
aware that the wasteful words were effortless.

(iv)

When Suniti's friends came upon her soliloquizing yet again, they felt they had better say something.

"Look here," they scolded. "Why do you want to be a saint? Why invent devils? Why write poetry?"

"Writing poetry is what human beings do," Suniti was patient. "It's like birds, you know. Poetry is the sound of the human animal."

She had said this with such complete conviction, that her friends were silenced, but only for a moment.

"Okay, but why don't you write about concrete, everyday things? Why all this mythicism?"

"Because," replied Suniti, "an ordinary person going on and on about angels and devils, that, don't you see, is the human condition."

"Well, but" – her friends were unconvinced – "why don't you do something really useful? Take up a trade. You'd feel a lot better."

"This is my trade!" Suniti snapped. She was getting indignant.

Her friends realized they had gone too far. "Oh. Well, here we all are. Ply your trade. Entertain us."

"That's exactly what I have been doing," Suniti retorted.

Her friends were startled. They did not feel in the least entertained, but they tried again.

"Well, instruct us as well. Give us some answers."

Suniti was exasperated. "I have just defined the human condition, and for good measure I've even thrown in the nature of poetry. You too have a part to play, you know." She glared at them earnestly, "You have a function."

With that she shut her eyes, opened her mouth, and began to recite. Her friends were not really unkind at heart, they listened politely. During a pause one of them whispered, "Now are we behaving like proper humans?"

Manuscript broken off.

14 May 1991

I wrote this poem 21 years ago. Verse is useless. Prose no better. List the headlines: Famine in Africa, The Plight of the Kurds, The Cyclone in Bangladesh. Why has it happened? Why do these things happen over and over and over again?

Nov. 1970 CYCLONE IN PAK.

100,000 human beings
were swallowed by sea
in a single day
and then thrown up,
because
2000 miles of polluted oil
have made the sea
less than tolerant.
"Think of the loss," they said,
"visualize in numbers.
Sea-sodden corpses
are useful to no one.
200,000 eyeballs
never to be grafted.
100,000 heads of hair
spoilt by sea-water.
Next time it happens
we'll have a freezer handy.
Next time a battery
of poets will be ready."

The poets are not ready. Unlike Canute, I didn't think that a poem, a word or two, could hold the sea in, but *it should not have happened*. What is the use of these breaks in the manuscript? Any fool could have told me that life doesn't happen in ways that can be enclosed in a poem. Poems happen in ways that can be enclosed by life? A detail on the canvas – a poet mouthing in the face of disaster? Is there something inherently indecent about trying to write verse?

X

The Ubiquitous Lout

Grendel's Ma, annoyed and amazed that Suniti had somehow set herself up and begun to acquire a reputation, if not as a saint then at least as someone with a serious purpose, decided to teach her a lesson. At the dead of night, she rose from the slime, walked through the streets, with, as usual, Grendel in tow – who could get rid of that ubiquitous lout? – and woke up Suniti. At this stage in her meanderings, Suniti had decided that if she couldn't save her soul, and if she couldn't quite bring herself to lose it either, then she would try to preserve her life. And so, when Grendel's Mum and her pale offspring appeared at her bedside, Suniti immediately seized a knife and brandished it in the face of terror.

Grendel's Ma was taken aback. "It's only me and Grendel. Put that knife away. What has happened to your saintly pretensions?"

"Given them up," Suniti retorted. "What are you doing here?"

Grendel's Mum adjusted fast. "Just dropped by," she

replied pleasantly. "Maybe now that you've changed, you and I have something in common?"

Suniti didn't know what to say. Grendel's Ma as friend and ally? She fumbled for her specs, and examined the monsters. In this dim half-light they looked normal. Still, caution was needful. "I do not like uninvited visitors," she informed them sternly.

But Grendel's Ma appeared unoffended. "Well, invite us then. We'll behave ourselves. You'll soon see that you can count on us." She smiled at Suniti.

Suniti failed to smile back. "What? Him as well?" She was staring at Grendel in open dismay. He had taken to scuffing and kicking the carpet. Suniti peered at his trail through the door. Muddy footprints. Mud and slime. She glared at his mother, who met her glare and seemed not to be in the least discomposed.

"Him too." Mama was firm.

Suniti didn't know what to do. Her new resolutions hadn't prepared her for this. In her mind's eye she had worked out strategies, survived sieges and fought many battles; but what was she to do with friendly aliens?

"Well, I'll think about it," she muttered at last. She knew that at best it was a feeble response; but daily life with well-meaning monsters – was it possible? She dismissed them wearily, "Now, please go." She sank upon her pillows.

But as Grendel and his Ma shambled through the door, she called out to them. "If you want to be friends, you'll have to tell the truth. What did you come for?"

Grendel's Ma, paused for a second. "To show you up," she answered briefly over her shoulder.

All the next day Suniti tried to write about light and life, about flowers that bloom in the pale air; but all she could think about was Grendel's Mum. In the end she gave up and wrote boldly across a piece of paper: I WILL WRITE ABOUT GRENDEL'S MUM.

But Grendel's Mum sounded so ordinary. She began again. I WILL WRITE ABOUT THE MOTHER OF EVIL. But that would make Grendel evil, Evil Incarnate, Supreme Evil. Did he qualify? Who was Grendel? She thought about Grendel, and came to the conclusion that Grendel was merely a pusillanimous lout. She loathed Grendel. But Grendel's Mum? Why had she given birth to Grendel? What was the link? The missing connection?

And what did Mum want from her? Why visit her? They had crept up on her in the middle of the night. If they had really wanted to rip her to shreds, they could have done it easily. She'd been asleep. Why wake her up? Why visit? Why her?

After a while she began to wonder what it would be like to be Grendel's Mum. Should she write that? I WAS MONSTER'S MUM. The child is mother of the man. . . That would sell. Or better still: I WAS MONSTER MUM. But that had been done. That had been done over and over by Grendel and his like. But if the Grendels of this world hated their Mum, then was she not on the same side as all the little Grendels? They had a common cause. And what about Mum?

Grendel and his Mum were not pleasing subjects. Now that she had given up her saintly aspirations, was it really necessary to wade in mud? Why think about Grendel? Why even consider the possibility of making friends with monsters?

Nevertheless, she wrote a little note: might she visit them? And if so, what time would be most convenient? Having sent it off, she felt better. She settled down to work. Neatly and clearly she wrote across her piece of paper: The Descent into Hell. Then she waited for life to happen. It didn't take long. In no time at all, she heard Mama roaring across the rooftops, "Come any time. We're ready and waiting. We're at your disposal!"

Armed with disgust and an immense intolerance, Suniti slipped and slithered through the mud. The slime crept about her. The slime transfigured her. She probably looked like Grendel's Mum. She was Grendel's Mum? In panic she fell and groped in the mud: where was her sense of heroic purpose? Deep from her throat, rage and resentment boiled out of her.

Slime slithers from my body.
My weeping flesh balloons and bloats.
Grendel creeps in my belly.
Why should I keep the Monster afloat?

Why complain?
All this is merely natural process.
Creatures live, and eat, and die.
Some few must feed from your weary flesh.

But to claim kinship?
Are the maggots mine? The slime –
mine? Is the divine
right to feed and be fed
– is that also mine?

It's lonely in hell.
Your verse disintegrates.
But look around you.
Your friends are all here,
Your hurts and your hates.

The sluggard and his mother?
My brother and his other?
Why are they here?
Let them disappear!
Why can't I live in a private hell?

It is your own. This you have made.
Here you are king and you are maid.

Your hurts and your hates
*   are these stuttering shades.*
Your "privacy" is well
*   respected in hell.*

Summon a shade.
    I'll be the judge of what I've made.
If they gibber and squeak,
    I'll bellow and yell and make them speak.

You cut out their tongues.
*   You said it was just. They suffer as well.*
Now lend them your voice.
*   They too (as you know) have a tale to tell.*

The denizens of hell flutter about me
    like lunatic sparrows.
I sit cat-like
    and spurn these feathered arrows.

Speak for the frantic.
*   They are striving to charm.*
Can you not see?
*   They mean you no harm.*

I do not believe it.
    Given a chance
They'd put out my eyes
    And further advance.

Then fear the bitter monsters.
  Not one of them will speak.
They'll growl and they'll groan,
  They'll grunt and they'll shriek.

Do you think I'm afraid?
I, who was once the Conquering Maid?

You are composed of fear.
Perhaps you like it? You hold it dear.

Very well, then. I'm willing to treat.
If I should die, it's *your* defeat.

I showed you my bones. I offered my need.
You said I was composed of dearth and deceit.

Who said that?
Thin-boned sparrow?
Or ravenous cat?

You raged at me so righteously
and said you were no enemy.

You wept in my arms. I held you dear.
You chose in my stead the shape of your fear.

My mere minor vices did you no harm.
Can foolish devices engender alarm?

You metamorphosed me, said I was vile,
I, a poor, pitiful, puling child?

They charm the ear.
     They lie with skill,
          And wait until
The ear is closed,
     Then,
          Kill, Kill, Kill.

O mirror mirror on the wall,
Who is the cleverest of us all?
   She, said the sparrow,
   with her bow and her arrow.
She hath taught the sparrow to fall.

I am not cleverer than you.
You've entered my brain, and body too.
You win, I lose.
Teach me
         (since you must)
                 What must I do?

She knows the right answer.
O the blithe and bitter dancer.
She knows and won't say.
   She wants a holiday.
   She don't want to pay.
   She wants to go away.
   She don't want to pray.

She says she's gone astray.
She's bleating (and cheating).
She's thinking of eating
(us up). She's taking a beating.
 That's only her way.
Her way of cheating. She should
(ask us to sup). She should let up.

You should let up. *You* should stop.
I'm down on my knees. Now tell me, please.
What must I do?

And all the little monsters said in a chorus:
You must kiss us.
What! You who are evil,
Ugly and uncivil.
You who are cruel,
Afraid and needy,
Uncouth and seedy.

Yes, moody and greedy.
Yes. You must bless us.

But the evil you do.
The endless ado.
Why bless you?
You are composed of such shameful stuff.

Because, said the monsters, beginning to laugh,
Because, they said, cheering up.
You might as well. You are part of us.

It crossed Suniti's mind that it would be nice now to fall down on the floor in a dead faint. Whatever she looked like, the body language would vindicate her: she would be a victim. And as a victim in a dead faint, it would be clear that she could do nothing, could not in any way be responsible. Unfortunately, her brain was working. In spite of the murk, in spite of the monsters, her mind was lucid. But to have to kiss the little monsters, all the little monsters rolled into one, to have to embrace their greed and their need and their murderous fear? Her brain revolted. She could not do it. And yet? She commanded her brain to command her arm. . . , some part of her commanded something to do something. She stretched out a hand. Grendel stared. Then he grabbed it and bit her finger. And Suniti? Suniti just stood there, startled that for once the ready response, the well-known surge of contempt and anger, had not invaded her.

Back in her study, she wrote on a clean sheet of paper:

> Love is the Law,
> > And Cruelty the Climate,
> > > Let the Cultures collide.

Then, neatly and methodically, she bandaged her finger.

XI

Songs of Despair

(i)

As sinless as lambs,
               forever the victims,
never perpetrating the slightest sin:
               would you like to be a lamb?
O tiger, tiger, burning bright,
               we respect the wages of sin.
Death, did you say? No, death postponed.
               Others shall die that I might win.

(ii) Natural History

Audubon paints a blue heron. I speculate on this. In the picture there's a paler, smaller bird. Is it an aspirant, a lesser creature hoping to achieve a Bluer Heronry? On the news today the Muslims are killing the Serbs again and the Serbs are killing the Muslims back. A clever monkey has overrun the planet. Death to other species. The male monkey has some unpleasant habits. The female of the species is more subdued; but experiments have shown that given the chance (and a little encouragement) she'll kill with a will. Some of these monkeys (including the killers) are able to write little songs. Some of these monkeys are charmed by herons, bats and butterflies, diverse species. Some of the time some of these monkeys seize the occasion to write elegies.

22 April 1992

(iii)

Somewhere among the powers that have been
there must be a god, a goddess, a godling,
somebody friendly. Ah no, somebody beautiful,
kind, tender, true: a goddess who might say,
"Suniti? What troubles you now?
                              Who wrongs you?"
And would she embrace me then?
                              Or would I, Suniti,
then have to be kind, tender, beautiful, true. . .

XII

On the Extinction of Dragons

The dragon and Suniti are bleeding to death. Grendel and Mum stand by as mourners, but there is no urgency: a slow death can occupy a lifetime.

"Shall we shake hands?" the dragon mutters. "Shall we be reconciled?"

"To what purpose," Suniti replies. "For whose benefit? Who is observing us?"

"Them?" ventures dragon, thumb stuck out in the general direction of Grendel and Mum.

"No, you are Grendel. I'm his Mum," S replies wearily. "Haven't you understood that?"

"No, you are Grendel. I'm his Mum." The dragon too sounds weary.

For a little while they bleed in silence.

"What about the others?" the dragon asks.
"Who?"

"Oh, the angel who didn't give you £20,000, the gilded lilies, the poetry-listening friends, the candidates for sainthood, the lion and the lamb."

"Tiger," corrects Suniti.

"Yes, tiger. And the irises and the poppies and the mute serpent. And the sparrow. Don't forget the sparrow."

"Oh they carry on, until such time as they fail to carry on."

More silence.

The dragon has been contemplating his own death. "Don't you think that the extinction of dragons would be a very sad thing?"

No answer.

After a while the dragon ventures, "I've composed an elegy."

"Why?"

"That's what poets do."

"And saints?"

"They do the same thing, only they do it with their lives."

S frowns. It's a pretty good answer; she wishes she had thought of it.

"Well, be elegiac," she snaps suddenly. "Why don't you recite?"

The dragon begins. "It's for you," he says softly.

"That night no nightingale said a word.
Ordinary birds,
busy racketing all the day long,
strangely
forgot their ebullience, and walked
rather than flew
and chirrupped not at all. Something
long-awaited
– a reasonable conjecture – was surely
about to occur.
The leaves stopped rustling, the jasmine
held her breath,
and even the cat, who was conveniently asleep,
buried herself
in a greater drowsiness. Then, into that garden,
as casually
as moonlight, eternity crept, and thereafter, death."

Suniti doesn't know what to say.

"Do you want me to die?" She blurts it out.

And like any poet, the ready answer, "That *wasn't* my point!"

Eventually, a bird starts up, leaves rustle. In between these sounds, the sound of the dragon: "But wouldn't the extinction of dragons be very sad?"

Part Two

The Solidarity Fables

Lost Leader

A hedgehog who had been pampered and privileged early in life decided one day that it was her obvious destiny to become the most refined hedgehog the world had ever known. Were there any precedents? She dipped into the literature on the nature of hedgehogs. 'Hedgehogs are creatures of the night,' she read. 'Hedgehogs eat insects, but will eat almost anything, including carrion.' 'Hedgehogs –' sometimes she got so cross that she found it difficult to carry on, but she persevered. 'Hedgehogs lie about and spend half their time sleeping underground.' Once she came across a picture of a hedgehog with raggedy looking leaves stuck all over her. The caption indicated that the hedgehog had deliberately rolled in the leaves, presumably in order to keep herself warm. The Refined Hedgehog slammed the book shut. "Right," she said. "I am going to enlighten them."

She called a meeting in broad daylight and prepared a feast of delicate flowers and bunches of grapes in varying hues of blue and purple. At about 2 o'clock three hedgehogs arrived and stood there uncertainly blinking at her. She did her best to make them feel at home. Half an hour later a few more straggled in. The Refined Hedgehog clambered up a rock. She glared briefly and then she shouted, "Hedgehogs are wonderful!"

For a moment or two nothing happened, then one of the hedgehogs understood what she had said and took up the cry. The rest followed. The Refined Hedgehog smiled to herself. She glared at the hedgehogs once again. "Hedgehogs enjoy the best things in life!" The hedgehogs were learning. They fell upon the grapes with a great deal of grabbing and grunting and larking about. The Refined Hedgehog was a little less pleased, but she waited for her guests to finish eating. It didn't take long. She glanced about her. The garden was a mess and it looked as though some of the hedgehogs were thinking of leaving. She shouted quickly, "It's Time We Came Out!" The response overwhelmed her. As the assembled hedgehogs streamed out of the gate and onto the streets, the Refined Hedgehog was jostled and pushed and trodden upon.

She lay where she had fallen, telling herself that she ought to join the others; but as they marched down the street she saw that more and more hedgehogs were Coming Out. She stayed where she was and nursed her bruises, then, very, very softly, so that nobody could hear her, she whispered to a leaf, "Hedgehogs are not wonderful." A little while later, after she had had time to recover, she confided cautiously to another leaf, "Not all hedgehogs are always wonderful." Time went by. The Refined Hedgehog lived quietly. She had lost her ambition and seldom went out. Nevertheless, as it happened, she did go down in history, not quite as she had intended, but as the Legendary Leader and First Casualty of the Hedgehog Cause.

Manners

Once upon a time a bright red fish crept about on the ocean floor, sidled past seaweeds and apologized if any other fish so much as looked at her. When asked what it was she was apologizing for, she humbly replied that it was for occupying space. She irritated everyone. But on the whole it was felt that if she chose to sidle rather than swim, then this was after all a minor eccentricity and hurt no one. And so she sidled and slithered as much as she liked and prided herself on her excellent manners, until one day she met a bully. "What are you sliding and slithering for?" demanded the bully. Whereupon the red fish was so overcome that she tipped over on one fin and floundered in the mud. "Well?" growled the bully. "Oh," gasped the red fish, "oh." These pitiful sounds were not hard to interpret – with a little trouble. They seemed to say, 'Oh that I, who am so distinguished for an exquisite courtesy, should be treated so.' But the bully took no trouble. The bully simply occupied space and watched with what looked like superb confidence. The red fish writhed. She writhed and wriggled and buried herself deep in the mud. And the bully smiled: at least the red fish had tidied up after herself, and left no trace of an awkward existence.

O Red Bird of Paradise

The really unusual birds in the entire forest were the red ones with two green wings. It wasn't that they were freaks or even mutants or stray representatives of an exotic species, or anything like that. It was just that all the other birds in the forest had green bodies with two red wings or green bodies with two green wings or red bodies with two red wings or yellow wings or purple wings or some other combination which went unnoticed. It was only the red birds with green wings who were considered unique. "You are unique," someone would say to one of the red birds. "Oh no," the red bird would reply. "Have you met my sister? She is like me." "Well, yes," the bird would be told. "She too is unique. Let's not quibble. The fact remains that birds like you are extraordinary." "Well, yes," the bird would assent. "That is so. That has always been so. We are used to it." And so really there was no problem. Everyone was agreed that the birds were unique, until one day a zoologist came along who treated the birds as though they were ordinary. This caused consternation. "Haven't you realized," someone said to the zoologist, "that these birds are extraordinary, while the rest of us are ordinary?" "Oh no," replied the zoologist, "these birds are very, very ordinary." Everyone was flabbergasted. "But they don't act ordinary." "No," said the zoologist. "And the rest of us do." "Yes," said the zoologist. "Well, what does it mean?" "I think it means," replied the zoologist, "that being extraordinary is an acquired characteristic."

The Promise of King Hilar

When King Hilar fell off his horse in the middle of the forest and sprained his ankle, he was so grateful to the woman who rescued him that he promised her the thing he treasured most. The woman didn't pay any attention to this. All she saw was that he was hurt and needed help. Whether or not he was the King Hilar didn't matter to her. She was happy enough living in the forest and didn't need anything much or promises of things from anyone. And so when the courtiers had been sent for and the king had been rescued and taken care of, she forgot all about him.

But the king didn't forget. He took himself very seriously indeed and felt strongly that a royal promise ought not to be broken. He lay on his couch and thought hard. 'Shall I give her my emerald bowl or my golden sword or my silver studded saddle or my beautiful carpet with all the beasts of the forest woven on it in silken threads of a thousand different colours, or shall I give her. . .?' He became confused. He summoned the Royal Treasurer. "Read out a list of all my treasures," the king commanded him. "Certainly, Your Highness," answered the treasurer, "but it would take weeks and weeks." A promise was a promise, but the king didn't want to spend weeks on it. He frowned at the treasurer. "Listen," he told him, "just reel off the names of half a dozen treasures I happen to own." The treasurer said quickly, "Well, Your Majesty, there are the 2 riding camels, the 3 elephants – 2 black and 1 white – and the Arabian racehorse. There are also –" "That will do," interrupted the king. "Now send off someone to summon the woman." "What woman, Your Majesty?" asked the treasurer timidly. "The woman who rescued me, of course," growled the king. Then he lay back and pretended to sleep because his ankle was hurting him.

The courtiers rode into the forest and brought back the woman who had helped the king. She was a little annoyed at being disturbed in this way, but tried to be nice. The king smiled at her expansively, "Now, dear lady, I have among my possessions 2 black elephants, 1 white, 2 riding camels and a thoroughbred horse. Which of these would you like for yourself?"

"None of them, Your Majesty, though it's kind of you to offer. You see, I live in a small house in the middle of the forest. Where would I put them? And what would they eat?"

"Oh. Well, is there something else you would like instead?"

"Nothing, thank you, Your Majesty," the woman replied.

At this, His Majesty became petulant. "But don't you see, you're getting in the way of a king keeping his solemn promise. Do try to help. Isn't there anything at all that you would really like?"

The woman thought. "Well," she murmured at last. "I would really like a cup of tea."

"Is that all?" The king was disappointed. "That's too easy."

"But that's what I want," replied the woman. "And you have to make it."

"Oh," said the king. He summoned the Royal Chef. "How," he asked, "do you make a cup of tea?" The Royal Chef explained in detail. "Oh," said the king again. "Well, fetch me some fire and some water and a few tea leaves." Then the king limped about and finally produced a weak cup of tea. He handed it to the woman who had waited patiently through all this fuss. "Thank you," she said. She drank it politely, and then returned to the forest where she lived happily.

Two Ducks and a Tortoise

In the course of a long and lazy summer two ducks and a tortoise became excellent friends. When autumn came they continued friends. But as the days grew shorter and the nights colder, and there were chunks of ice floating about, the ducks became more and more moody. The tortoise thought that she had offended them. She was very sorry. "Please," she said, "whatever it is I've done or not done, it was entirely unintentional. Can't we be friends?"

"But we are friends," the ducks replied and fluffed their feathers and did their best to look pleasant.

"But we no longer swim and play and dive underwater as we used to before," the tortoise insisted. "You've been avoiding me of late. Please. What have I done wrong?"

"Oh," said the ducks pulling themselves together. "Oh. It's not you at all. It's just the – the nature of things, the nature of reality, the way ducks are when winter comes."

The tortoise didn't understand. She felt lonely and miserable. The ducks for their part were also unhappy. They didn't know how to break it to her that they would have to leave soon.

"We could just stay here and freeze to death," said one duck to the other.

"But after we were dead, she would still feel lonely and still feel bad," replied the other.

"True," said the first and dropped the argument.

The two ducks shivered and scowled and scowled and shivered and in the end they agreed to tell the tortoise the truth since they couldn't think of anything else to tell her.

The tortoise was brooding on a rock by herself. The ducks approached her. "Look," they blurted out, "if we don't leave soon, we'll freeze to death."

"Is that all?" asked the tortoise.

"What do you mean – is that all? It's a serious matter. Didn't you hear us? We're freezing to death."

"Oh yes, but the solution is simple. I'll go with you."

"What?" said the ducks.

"I'll go with you," repeated the tortoise.

And so the three friends devised a sling which they attached to a pole. The tortoise climbed into it. The ducks picked up the ends of the pole in their strong beaks and they all flew away together in short hops. In the summer they returned, and this they did year after year until, at last, they decided to retire and settled in the south.

That Shaggy Look

The wild mare had come to the moors so long ago that she had almost forgotten why it was she had originally walked out; but here was her niece standing before her expecting to be given the right answers.

"It was because you were fed up with bourgeois respectability and creature comforts, wasn't it?" her niece demanded.

The wild mare hesitated. Living as she did on the moors, she had learned to appreciate warmth and shelter, not to mention food and water; besides, as best as she could remember she had never had anything against creature comforts, and as for bourgeois respectability she wasn't quite sure what it was.

Luckily her niece hadn't noticed that she hadn't answered. "And, of course, that shaggy look is a form of protest," her niece went on.

This was too much. The wild mare had never been vain, but she had never thought of herself as a sloven. "Do you mean my long hair?" she asked stiffly. She wanted to explain that it was difficult to get it trimmed and that moreover it kept her warm.

"Yes," her niece broke in. "Look, I've copied the style. Do you think it suits me? It's very much the fashion, since these days you are the fashion."

"What do you mean?"

"Your ideas and everything. Thank you for explaining them. I shall tell everyone when I get back."

"But I haven't explained anything," the mare cried out.

"Of course you have. All that you said about doing without and wearing your hair long – it's really caught on. Well, I must go now."

Her niece left, while the wild mare stood stock still and pondered the point that in the course of time she had gained acceptance, if not as an individual, then certainly as a tourist attraction.

Wolf

There was once a young woman who made friends with a wolf. At first the men were filled with admiration. "It's because she's a virgin," they would whisper slyly. "Look, how even the wild beasts fear her. She has tamed the wolves." All this was nonsense, of course. There had never been any question of taming. It was simply that the woman and the wolf got on, and frequently went for walks together. But as time went by and the virgin continued to remain a virgin, and the wolf continued to remain a wolf, the men became peevish. "The fact is," they explained to one another, "she uses the wolf to guard her virginity. The man who would win her must slay the wolf." The story spread, the hunters got ready and a great wolf-hunting expedition was organized. The virgin was asked to serve as bait. "That isn't good sense," the virgin protested; but the hunters said that they were in charge and understood these matters. In the end they tied the virgin to a tree in the forest and hid among the bushes. They waited for the wolf. No sign of a wolf. By the following morning they were tired and hungry so they returned to their houses and slept all day. At night they were back. Still no wolf – and no virgin either. A sure sign, they told one another, of the presence of wolves. All night long they ranged through the forest. They grew tired. They fell asleep in the forest. They woke up and hunted and fell asleep again. They were thoroughly lost, but night after night they hunted for virgins and also for wolves. In the end the elders decided that the forest had swallowed them, so they put up a sign on the edge of their town in large red letters warning the unwary that there were wolves about.

Subsequent History

The subsequent history of the young woman and that of
the wolf is harder to trace. Once they had eluded the
hunters, they looked at one another ruefully. "Perhaps
some other country, some other village . . ." muttered
the wolf. They were tired and wanted to rest. But the
first set of villagers they came upon hemmed and
hawed and finally said well, all right, they could stay
provided the wolf was thoroughly examined and had
every tooth and claw removed. When they approached
the next village the wolf tried hard to look as harmless
as possible, but this lot weren't interested in the wolf.
They told the young woman that it was necessary for
her to marry one of them and settle down at once. And
so the two friends walked away and when at the third
village they were rudely greeted by sticks and stones,
because, it was claimed, their reputation had preceded
them, they were not greatly surprised, but just walked
on until, at last, they entered a realm that is not as yet
familiar to us.

Ordinary Ears

It so happened that a sow gave birth to seven little piglets with bright red ears. At first the sow was startled, but as the piglets were born one by one she got used to it. And so when the eighth and last piglet was born with perfectly ordinary ears, she was a little put out. She had thought she had produced a distinguished litter. She examined the piglet carefully, she noted its habits and play patterns, but it showed no signs of being exceptional. She worried about it and in the end she confided in her sister. "It's little Ordinary Ears. I've checked the weight charts, I've checked the height charts, and the number of hours she spends rooting about. She conforms to the norm in every particular."

"Oh well," replied her sister. "There's no need to worry. It's not given to every little piglet to stand out, you know. It's true that I've been lucky in my own little ones, but mediocrity is, after all, the salt of the earth."

Little Ordinary Ears' mother didn't care for this answer, but she didn't know what to say, so she said hastily, "Little Ordinary Ears isn't ordinary at all. That's not why I'm worried. The truth is she's very unusual."

"Oh?" murmured her sister.

"Yes," said the sow, trying to think rapidly. "There's

nothing wrong with her. It's just that she has a rare condition."

"Well, you had better take her to the doctors."

"No, no, it's nothing like that." Ordinary Ears' mother hesitated. "It's – it's just her ears."

"What about her ears?"

"They're made of the purest and most durable silk."

"What?"

"They are made of the purest and most durable silk. They are very delicate and soft. And it makes me afraid that some day somebody might snip them off."

Suddenly her sister smiled sympathetically. "Oh my dear, I feel for you. That's exactly my worry about my own little ones. Silken ears must run in the family. But after all, that is something that we can both be proud of."

"Yes," responded Ordinary Ears' mother. "We come of good stock."

Then the two sisters grunted in agreement and allowed themselves to enjoy the sun.

Schooling

Once upon a time there was a red fish with blue dots, absurd fins which stuck out on both sides like elephants' ears, and a spangled tail. The other, more ordinary grey fish informed her dispassionately that she was absurd – no two ways about it, she was indisputably and manifestly absurd. The red fish chewed her lower lip, sighed and agreed, well, yes, blue polka dots . . . a bright red colour . . . patently absurd, but was there anything she could do about it? "No, no," the grey fish said kindly. "There is nothing you can do. We were not suggesting that it was your fault." "You have misunderstood me," replied the fish. "I was not trying to expiate guilt. I was merely trying to change my appearance." "But would that be honest?" The red fish looked at the others in surprise. "Are you saying," she asked, "that I either have to be bad and beautiful or I have to be ugly and honest?" "Oh no, no, no. Heaven forbid that we should use such loaded language," they cried out in chorus. "Well, what are you saying then?" demanded the red fish. "We were merely commenting on your appearance." "What's wrong with it?" "Oh, there's nothing 'wrong' with it. It's just that it's a little –" "Yes?" "Foreign." In the end the red fish swam away, while the silvery fish glanced discreetly down their streamlined sides, their elegant backs, and shimmered.

Pelican

The Blue Donkey said, "I'll tell you a story."

"Oh good," said her disciples as they were supposed to do.

"There was once a pelican," the Blue Donkey began, "who had acquired a tremendous reputation for wisdom. Birds would fly across the length of the lake in order to consult her, and as the advice she gave was often sensible and always kindly, her reputation increased. Soon the lake became a place of pilgrimage and birds were flying in from all over the world for a bit of advice and a bit of sight-seeing. Things got crowded, but nobody much minded and the pelican continued modest and friendly. Then one morning a fish poked her head out of the water, and before she had finished saying, 'Please, O Pelican – ' the pelican had snapped her up and stored her in her beak. The fish continued speaking, 'Do you always eat up those who find themselves in trouble and come to you for help and advice?' The pelican wanted to say, 'Of course not!' but the fish was in her mouth and she couldn't speak. The fish went on, 'I am at this very moment in grievous difficulty. What is your advice?' The pelican wanted to say, 'Keep away from pelicans, O you silly fish.' But, of course, with her mouth full she still couldn't speak. 'Well?' insisted the fish. 'Persistent little beggar,' the pelican thought. She had got into the habit of giving advice and it bothered her that she couldn't give it.

'You've got a problem, haven't you?' continued the fish, who appeared to be a compulsive talker. 'It seems to me you have two choices. You could swallow me up and obviate my need for kindly advice together with my need for a kindly pelican, or you could spit me out and find out what it was I came for really.'

'I will let you go,' said the pelican, spilling out the fish even as she spoke. 'Now what did you come for?'

'I came to show that as far as fish are concerned your reputation as a sage is tarnished.'

'Oh,' said the pelican, 'that doesn't matter.'

'What do you mean ?' asked the fish.

'Well, you see,' said the pelican, 'I don't eat birds and to my fellow birds that's what matters.'

'But there are fish among us,' the fish cried out, 'who are willing to see pelicans as fellow fish.'

But the pelican just shrugged and ignored the fish."

The Blue Donkey paused and looked at her disciples earnestly, "Now, was the pelican evil?"

"No," they all said.

"Was the fish a fool?"

"Yes," they all said.

The Blue Donkey shook her head and frowned. "Now look," she admonished them. "Think properly. Whose side are you on?"

"Neither," replied the disciples taken by surprise. "We're not really interested in birds or fish."

The Blue Donkey frowned more fiercely. "That's not the right answer. Try once again."

The disciples thought hard. Then one of them ventured, "It really depends —"

"On what?"

"On whether the pelicans see the fish as fellow pelicans or simply as fish."

The Blue Donkey sighed. "Look. Let's simplify matters." She glared at the circle of little donkeys, "Are you pelicans or are you fish?"

"Both?" said the disciples anxiously, hoping that at last they'd got it right.

Higher Education

When two ducks came across a hippo, standing in the middle of their pathway to the Cam, they consulted one another about whether they ought to try to be nice. She is, after all, a stranger, they decided, and who knows they might some day find themselves on the shores of Africa and a helpful hippo would then prove to be a very good thing. This was unlikely, of course, but the thought of being nice to the hippo made them feel kindly and they liked the feeling. "Better teach her the rules," one of them murmured. "You're blocking the path," the other called out. The hippo lumbered on and dropped into the Cam. "No splashing allowed," the first duck yelled. "Bathing privileges conditional only." "Sorry," replied the hippo and submerged herself. The ducks waited for the hippo to reappear. They wanted to have a talk with her and explain everything. They waited half an hour, but nothing happened. "Do you think she's drowned?" one of them asked. They peered underwater, but the waters of the Cam were murky and muddy and they couldn't see a thing. Another half hour passed. No hippo appeared. The ducks began to feel cross and foolish. "Anyone would think that we had nothing better to do than to wait for hippos." They swam away downstream. After a while one of them said, "What do you suppose happened to the hippo? She just vanished." "It's just as well," the other replied. "She'd have probably found it hard to really fit in."

Calvin versus Darwin
versus the Penguin

"Consider the penguin," the Moralist informed whoever was listening. The penguin ignored her. After all, if the Moralist wanted to shiver and chatter on the remote shores of the cold Antarctic, that was her business; the penguin was considering a morning dip. "From the penguin we can learn," the Moralist waved in the direction of the penguin – rather rudely the penguin thought – "the dire consequences of giving way to a slothful impulse." The penguin stared. As far as she knew, she wasn't slothful. She paused for a moment. The Moralist went on, "There is no excuse. Not for anyone. No one by nature is born lazy. But consider the penguin – " another careless wave. The penguin gave up; she set off briskly towards the sea. "But consider the penguin," – the Moralist hadn't noticed that the penguin had left – "PENGUINS CANNOT FLY! Centuries of sloth have made the penguin CONGENITALLY INDOLENT." The Moralist finished on a note of triumph. Meanwhile, the penguin, encased in her evolved swimsuit, was flying through the waves on her adaptable fins and steering with her feet on the trackless ocean.

The Guitar Player

(Vermeer, Kenwood)

A girl played on her guitar and it so happened that someone passing by listened and fell in love with her. "Is it my music you love," inquired the girl, "or me?" The music continued, water from a fountain rose into the air and fell away. The listener thought hard and finally said, "I don't know. What is the right answer?" "Shan't tell you," replied the girl, "but that's not it," and she went on playing. Soon another passer-by happened to see her and also fell in love. "Is it me you love," inquired the girl, "or my guitar?" The second passer-by stared at the guitar, smiled at the girl and at last ventured to say, "Well, I don't know. It's a beautiful instrument. What is the right answer?" But she just said that that wasn't it, and went on playing.

The two passers-by were greatly perplexed. All night long the guitar music ran through their heads, and when they returned the next day it was perfectly obvious that they had both prepared their speeches. "I would love you," declared the first, "even if you could not play a note of music." "And I would love you," swore the second, "even if you did not own a guitar."

"You don't understand," replied the girl. "I am a

musician. Which me do you love, if you do not care about my music at all?"

"Oh," they said. "Did we give you the wrong answer?"

"Yes," replied the girl.

"Well, what is the right answer?"

"You must love me altogether, just as I am, all my gifts, all my possessions, everything I've been and ever shall be from now on."

"But that's impossible!" they cried out together.

"Yes," agreed the girl and chose a sad little tune to suit the occasion.

Horror Story

A barn owl who had moved into a new neighbourhood generally kept herself to herself; but since, for quite some time, owls had been a rarity there, the gossip and the rumours quickly began. 'She lives alone.' 'She sleeps all day.' 'She's out all night.' As a foundation to build upon, these pieces of information were more than sufficient. Soon the owl represented everything that was wicked and glamorous. One or two fledglings aspired to be owls, but most were content to titillate one another by hooting meaningfully and falling about.

The days went by, and though the owl was closely observed, she did nothing to add to her reputation. Her neighbours grew restless. Just one or two details would have been most helpful. A crow and a starling took it upon themselves to call on her. They chose a respectable hour and they knocked and knocked, but the owl failed to answer. They knew she was in, because the starling had heard the rustle of feathers. There were other attempts, all unsuccessful. It was the general feeling that something should be done, but no one was quite sure exactly what.

And then one day the owl flew away. When the birds realised that she had gone forever, there was great excitement. They finally decided on a course of action.

They invaded her stronghold, and found, as they'd expected, dozens and dozens of skeletal remains – not hidden discreetly, not stashed away neatly, but just lying about.

The Blackbird's Heart

"Hang your heart on a tree! Hang your heart on a tree!" an irascible old woman had once told a blackbird. And the blackbird had believed her. The blackbird had reasoned that high and hidden in a tree somewhere her heart would be sheltered. Then, when a cat leaped on her, the cat would discover that she had no heart and would let her go. Then, when a boy with a shotgun aimed at her breast, it wouldn't much matter. The pellets might lodge, or the pellets might shoot clean through her, but her heart, high and swinging on a tree somewhere would remain unpierced. But it so happened that this unfortunate bird fell most fiercely and unsuitably in love. Her heart was now demanded of her. She flew away quickly in search of it. She had hidden it away in the early spring, it was now November. The wind helped her, and the trees divested themselves with lavish abandon, but the blackbird whirled in uncertain circles. Each time she spied a red berry she thought it was her heart, but how could she be sure? In the end she gathered all the berries that she could find and dropped them one by one in the lap of her true love. "Choose one," said the blackbird. "But which one is your heart?" "I don't know," replied the blackbird. Then the blackbird's true love gobbled the berries, while the blackbird watched and fell completely and cleanly out of love.

A few remained. "Are any of these your heart?" But the blackbird had gone. The blackbird's sweetheart looked around her. Windy November was nearly over. She scooped up the berries and took them indoors for her tree at Christmas.

Art is Long etc.

And then it so happened that the bluebird built a nest of the softest and most variegated moss, chose and arranged the strands with an artist's concentration, and wove them together with dedicated skill. When all this was done, she laid a solitary egg. It could be argued that this was a puny effort, but that would have been quibbling and the merest malice. It was the sort of egg that fabulists have attempted again and again and again to describe. It came out of folklore and fairy-tales and millionaires' dreams. It was veined and translucent. It was warm and soothing. From any perspective it curved with clarity. It charmed the senses, and the variegated nest of the softest moss was its perfect setting. Then it hatched. Shards littered the immaculate floor. An untidy fledgling stretched its neck over the rim of the moss and shrieked its needs. Dirt obscured the precise colouring. But the fledgling thrived. And, as for the bluebird, though the daily drudgery exhausted her, she was pleased that her work had been allowed to live.

Australian Notebook

For Renate

There were three elements: the woman, the cockatoo, and me – a disembodied narrator observing them. The woman had a body; the cockatoo was rock, sheer white rock, flint veined with quartz; and the cockatoo was in there, neither awake, nor asleep, but probably content. The woman was standing in front of the rock face. I don't think she was praying, though in the white moonlight that might have been appropriate. She was just looking at it. I could see the bird. But what happened next wasn't really possible: wing feathers stirred. How can feathers be composed of solid rock? How can they stir? Wouldn't the rock crumble? The rock was crumbling, slivers of flint grinding against one another, sparks and noise filling the air. When the bird emerged it had a sulphur crest. So far so good. The bird bowed. The woman bowed back. Everything was seemly, till the woman and the bird began shrieking at each other. I turned away then. Mere observers have their limitations. I saw them take off. The woman and the bird? No, the two cockatoos, the cockatoo and her sister. It stands to reason. Flying women belong to the realm of myth and comic books. But sulphur-crested cockatoos racketing in the sky – that's observed reality. And I have not presumed to interpret them.

Auto/Biog.

Then the Black Butterfly, intrepid and unsteady, weaving her way through galactic daisies, must have felt as powerful and pointless as any spaceship.

"Whither bound, Black Butterfly?"

And the words, fragile and fragmented, came fluttering back: "To meet my Destiny."

Binocular vision, a wide-angled gaze and the selfless stance of a mere machine enabled me to record the flights and falls, the diversions and deviations, the heights and depths, of the space-bound queen. But to know the unknown sets, as it were, its own limits. She led, I followed, scrupulously refusing to think anything. No doubt she had instruments of her own on board. The look-alike stars were there for a purpose. *Her* instruments could deal with these. I freewheeled freely. Belief and disbelief, both suspended, I did my job. That too, perhaps, is a kind of destiny?

Kittiwake

A ship or two sailing slowly beneath her, one or two
icebergs seemingly innocuous, lying in wait – but what
did they ever do? – they merely stood there – were
observed by the kittiwake with a disinterestedness that
might have been the envy of scientists anywhere. It was
not in her nature to let markers so large, even when
unfixed, go unremarked. But ships could not be eaten,
and the ice would only splinter; they could not sustain
her. It was the interface of ocean and the cold blue air –
on which she herself circled – the pattern upon pattern,
the shifting and the sliding – was it the wind? – or was
it the water? – that held her enthralled. So that eye and
brain worked, scrambling and unscrambling, scanning
the waves, on wings so reliable, so steady and strong,
that no brain power was required, and none spared, to
attend to them. Every now and then the pattern held; then
– the arrow through the circles, the kittiwake triumphant,
the treasure retrieved, the scales glittering, the fish in her
beak, returning to her perch, to the watching and gliding
on smooth, blue air. This gull, this kittiwake, might have
been the envy of poets anywhere.

Beauty Incarnate and the Supreme Singer

For Oscar Wilde

"Look," said the wren to the iris. "I'm not a nightingale. You're not a rose. But we too have a tale to tell, a song to sing, that sort of thing."

The iris was startled. She hadn't noticed the wren. She was engaged in letting the sun shine through her translucent skin, shaping and concentrating so that she glowed blue, with here and there a deep purple, modulating into darkness. "What do you mean?" she said.

The wren was taken aback. She had thought that her meaning was clear. "Well," she began, "you are not Beauty Incarnate like the rose – "

"I am beautiful!" The iris was irritated.

"Well, yes, that's just what I was getting at," replied the wren. She hadn't meant to annoy the iris, just the reverse. "What I was saying was that I am not a Supreme Singer, and you, of course, are not a rose – "

"Don't want to be a rose!" snapped the iris.

"No, of course not," soothed the wren. "You are not a rose, but you are very beautiful, and I would very much like to sing your praises."

"Oh. Go ahead then, but I'm busy at the moment."

"It's not that simple." The wren explained, "Don't you remember? The nightingale sang all night long –"

"Not all night," said the iris firmly.

The wren ignored the interruption. " – with her heart pressed against a thorn – "

"I haven't any thorns." The iris gazed down her long, green stalk, her smooth green leaves, with a certain smugness.

" – and bled to death," the wren finished triumphantly.

"Why?" asked the iris, jolted at last into proper awareness.

"Because she was suffering. In order to sing you have to suffer," the wren told her.

"But you're not suffering, are you?"

"I am a little," replied the wren modestly.

"Are you going to bleed?" By now the iris was thoroughly alarmed.

"Not if you're nice."

"I am nice. I'm very nice," the iris assured the wren earnestly. "And please, you don't have to sing my praises. I don't really care for poetry much."

"Now you're being cruel."

"No, no. I am not cruel. And I am not a rose!" the iris protested.

But the wren wasn't listening. She had already begun her plaint.

By the River

For Virginia Woolf

One day when the summer raged so that each leaf shook and clanged like tinsel, the beautiful black mare and her mistress rode into the forest to bathe in the river. As the woman splashed and played in a pool that the river had made and the mare cavorted among the spears of grass, the magic of the place took hold on them.

"O mare," said the woman while droplets fell from her wet black hair, "I understand you now. It must be the virtue of the water of this river."

"And I understand you," responded the mare, turning her head in a curve so graceful that had anyone seen her, his heart must have broken at the beauty of the gesture. "But it can't be the river. It must be the grass I've just eaten."

For a while they disputed happily: the woman saying she hadn't nibbled so much as a blade of grass, and the mare protesting that she herself hadn't stepped into the river. Eventually the woman emerged and laid herself down on the grass, while the mare disported herself in the river water. Whether it was the grass or the river didn't much matter.

But what was it then that the two had in common? An observer might have said that they were both beautiful. An observer might have added that they were both desirable. But would he have noted that they liked one another?

One of Us

"We'll pay you," said the Chair of the Board of Directors.

"Thanks," replied the Blue Donkey without stopping to think. She had got so used to haggling and hedging and quibbling and cribbing about the matter of money that she had responded without thinking, but in a moment caution prevailed. "Pay me for what?"

"For writing a story that proves our point."

The Blue Donkey considered. "How much will you pay?"

"Fifty pounds."

It wasn't very much, but it was better than nothing. The Blue Donkey stopped hesitating. "What is your point?"

"That we're in the right, and that they're in the wrong." The Chair of the Board expounded further, "They're lying and cheating. They won't co-operate and they hinder us when they can. What's more they're breaking all the rules!"

"Which rules?" the Blue Donkey enquired.

"The rules of all civilized societies on earth!"

"Are they civilized?"

"No!"

"That explains it." The Blue Donkey sighed. "What you mean is that they're breaking your rules."

The Director shrugged. "It's the same thing." She looked the Blue Donkey straight in the eye. "Look here, which side are you on?"

"That depends," murmured the Blue Donkey.

The Director decided to change her tactics. She would reason with the donkey. "Don't you care," she asked, "about justice and humanity and the quality of life?"

When the Blue Donkey did not reply immediately, the Director went on, "The fact is, it's a human rights issue, and so, of course it follows that you're on our side. You see, you are one of us." She waved expansively to include the other board members.

The Blue Donkey stared at them. "Do you mean to say," she asked curiously, "that you see yourselves as a bunch of donkeys?"

"Of course not." The Director appeared unoffended. "But we do share the same values."

"I see," said the Blue Donkey. "So it's a question of values?"

The Director nodded.

"And of rights?"

The Director continued to nod vigorously. Then she looked at her watch and wrote out a cheque. She thrust it at the donkey. "And also of interests!" she concluded in triumph.

Blood and Water

When the disobedient daughters of the River Ganges
diverged publicly, proved deviant, and made it clear
that they wished to follow their own course, their
mother disowned them. Though unable to kill and to
kill quickly, she changed them all into pale, blue
flowers: five-petalled things, nondescript, no longer
doughty, merely demure, and without defence. "Go
where you please," she told them scornfully, "undis-
tinguished, unhonoured and unashamed." That last
epithet she hadn't quite meant to put in at all, but the
River Ganges was hardly inclined to unstitch her words
and the sentence remained.

Inch by inch the daughters of Ganga crept across the
earth. They were found everywhere and found no-
where, since no one ever troubled to look for them. A
cow or a goat might step on them, an ignorant child
might sometimes pluck them – until told by its parents
that these were only weeds; but on the whole they continued unnoticed and safe. Centuries passed, the worship
of Ganga fell out of fashion. Men dismissed her as a
once mighty river, now reduced, and no longer a source
of gain or grain. And the river herself began to understand that even a god must suffer disgrace. News that is
no news spreads slowly. Though the daughters of Ganga

had travelled everywhere, they had carefully avoided their own birthplace. They began to return. Only the blue of their pale petals and their sudden reappearance gave them away.

"Can we help you, mother?" they asked quietly. Immersed as she was in her own despair, Ganga did not hear them. With the last of her passion she was pleading for death. And the daughters saw death approach. Was it their pity or merely the weakness of a dying goddess that broke those bonds so long imposed? With a sound like the shattering of millions upon millions of glass petals, the Daughters of Ganga flooded the riverbed.

The Function of Friendship

"What is friendship? What is sisterhood?" Regan demanded of her friend the poet. In her profundity Regan was intent on the meaning of things. "For example," she went on, "you and I are friends. But what does it mean?"

Her friend laughed. "It means," she replied, "a commonality of interests, and mutual trust and mutual esteem."

Regan considered. Did her friend then regard her with proper esteem? That was as it should be. But she had answered so quickly. Did she know the right answer? And why had she, Regan, not thought of it? No, her friend was too glib.

"Surely a difference of interests would vitiate the friendship," Regan murmured, and smiled. It was a smile she might have shed on a favourite pupil. Unfortunately, the favoured one's attention had wandered. She was admiring the roses. Regan sighed. How make her understand that Regan's concern was with the essentials of things? Something dramatic and definitive was necessary. Should she reveal her secret power? And could she both reveal and conceal it?

"Listen," she called out. "Do you see that mirror hanging on the wall?"

Her friend turned around. "No," she answered in her simplicity.

Regan stood up and indicated the mirror. "Pretend there's a mirror," she commanded her friend. "Look into it and listen carefully. Then tell me what you hear and what you see."

The friend obliged. She pretended to look and pretended to listen, she grinned. "The mirror says that you are the fairest of us all," she told Regan happily.

Regan understood that the poet was only teasing. She hid her annoyance. "Look," she said. "I'll show you how to do it." She walked up to the wall and looked into the mirror. "Now," she called. "What do you see?"

"A wall," replied her friend, who had tired of the game, "and you looking at it."

In cold anger Regan retreated to her couch again. "You are no poet! You see nothing!"

It was a dismissal. Her friend rose to go. In the doorway she paused. "Please," she asked hesitantly, "what was it I was supposed to see?"

Regan's answer sliced the silence. "Truth. Truth holding up a mirror to Justice." The closing door finalised it.

Social Theory

The Zoo must be run at a Healthy Profit. The Director
of the Zoo pondered the edict. The elephants and the
camels could always give rides. That was fair enough.
And £10 a go could be charged for attempting the wild
ponies, with a £50 prize for anyone who lasted for more
than 5 seconds. (Lawyers had been consulted and the
Zoo was not liable for broken bones.) Perhaps a fee could
be charged (to be collected in advance) for permission
to enter the lions' den? There were possibilities there...
but the monkeys remained a serious problem. They were
neither trained and tamed, nor raging and rabid. They
were merely untidy and fairly expensive. They ate quite
a lot; they were consumers, so to speak, rather than
producers; and it was increasingly clear that structure
was required. The monkeys must be patterned, must
learn to perform, must somehow become superbly
aesthetic, or at least orderly, must learn to charm, at
least not alarm, and above all they must earn their keep.
Ladders were the answer. Instead of ropes and tyres
strewn about haphazardly, ladders were introduced. And
the monkeys conformed. They climbed up the ladders,
they took up their stations; they formed a hierarchy and
vied for position. The Monkey House was formally
opened. What caused the riot, and who it was who threw

the first stone, whether it was a monkey or an onlooker pre-empting precisely that possibility, was never ever properly established; nor was it clarified whether the monkeys escaped or whether they were thrown out or whether, in fact, they were secretly removed to less expensive quarters. There was, however, a clear consensus that tenders for the property should be invited forthwith.

Gracefully for Grebes

"The Giant Crab is at least as big as a large elephant or a small house," the red-necked grebe was telling her friend. "I mean there it is, as large as life, just sitting there quietly at the bottom of the lake, pretending to be fast asleep. But it's really lying in wait for grebes."

"How do you know? Did you talk to it?"

"Of course not. It had a sign on its back: 'I EAT GREBES.' What could I have said to a creature that eats grebes?"

"Well, but we eat crabs," her friend pointed out.

"Yes, but a grebe eating crab is an entirely different matter from a grebe-eating crab. There's a difference in syntax, a difference in logic. One trips off the tongue and is clearly in keeping with the laws of nature, and the other is obviously an anomaly."

"This Anomaly – do you think we could kill it?" asked her friend.

The red-necked grebe shook her head sadly. "No, we'll have to opt for the peace offensive, and do it gracefully."

Whereupon the red-necked grebe was appointed by the grebes to dive into the lake and inform the Crab that henceforth no grebe, under any circumstances, would, in any way, ever attack any crustacean that was, in the slightest degree, its superior in size.

Mother Goose, Sister Goose and the Market-Led Farmer

The goose who laid golden eggs was hardly singular. She had a sister who could also lay eggs, silver ones or golden, plain ones or speckled – the ability had been inherited – but this sister had flatly declined. "Eggs hatch," she explained lazily. "Goslings grow up. But it's a long and tedious business, and on the whole, you see, I had rather do without." Her sister shrugged; but despite their differences, they remained good friends. They spent time together, they flew about together; and so, it's hardly surprising that when a trap was set for them, they were captured together. The farmer could hardly believe his good fortune when the following morning he found a golden egg, and all week long another and another. At the end of the week he decided to kill both the geese: one because she hadn't laid eggs, and the other because she had so profusely and splendidly done so. Then he'd be rich, the geese would be dead – wouldn't require feeding – and, in fact, he would be able to feed on them. The sisters overheard him. They pecked desperately at the wire netting until they managed to make their escape. Once they were safe and far away enough, they settled on a lake and looked at one another. "What does it mean?" muttered one of them. "Should we or shouldn't we?" "We should," said the other. "We shouldn't," replied the the first. They began squabbling. They made such a racket that two or three geese who were feeding nearby swam up to them. "Should or shouldn't what?" they asked the two sisters. "Make war on farmers," they replied together.

Bluebeard's Way

The truth is that Bluebeard was a miser. He hoarded gold, he hoarded furniture, and – yes, why not? – he hoarded women. After all, economists say that from the male point of view cows and women are a form of property. He did not hoard cows. Cleaning up shit, the problems of space, the awkwardness of size, in short, the logistics, just weren't worth it. And, in any case, he considered women the superior species. His house was honeycombed with hundreds of cells, and in each of these cells his women were fed and fattened and tran-quillized according to need.

The ownership of property is a serious matter, and the price of property is eternal vigilance. Bluebeard worked hard. He attended to his women twice a day, once in the morning and once each evening. The analogy to milking was constantly in mind, and also to farming, to digging, to ploughing, to hoeing, and to all that pertained to animal husbandry. His methods were efficacious and the women fertile, with the result that Bluebeard prospered. Male offspring were disposed of at birth; but the females he kept; and each was locked in an individual cell as soon as it was worthwhile.

But even Bluebeard could not hoard time. Time passed, time got spent whether or not Bluebeard allowed it. And in the course of time Bluebeard grew old. What of his property? Who would tend it? Who would do the milking ? Who would replace the old and the worn with the young and the new? Above all, who would appreciate the extent of his achievement and value it? The next male was allowed to live. As young Bluebeard grew to manhood, the old man witnessed a remarkable thing. Whereas he himself had had to coax and cajole and occasionally cuff his herd of cows, for the barely bearded boy the cows performed all that was required and much, much more, quite willingly. Old Bluebeard was vexed and perplexed. Ought he to be pleased? Was this indeed a measure of his success, or did it somehow reflect on him?

To the day of his death he could not decide, but die he did. And Young Bluebeard? He prospered. He was, as it were, a more mannerly man. Had he not been nurtured on kindness and milk? More male heirs were permitted to live, not just as a matter of mere kindness, but out of necessity. The farmhouse grew into a manor in his time, and then into a castle. By the time Bluebeard's grand-sons assumed the burdens of power, prestige and prosperity, the old man had become a fairy-tale figure. The methods he had used were systematized. Surplus males were organized in bands and asked to kill – one another that is. Survivors who by surviving had proved their pedigree were given some property – to look after that is. Eventually one or two lordlings managed to break away. There were battles and sieges and damage to property. The damage to property would have grieved the Old Man, but by now he had acquired the status of a central myth, and lies grew about him fast and freely. It was said, for example, that he had married his women one by one and killed them off sequentially. Others declared he had never married. And still others maintained that at the time of his death there was a general slaughter and a great bonfire marked the end of all his wives. There were disagreements about his doctrine and his deeds, but about his bearded image there was no squabbling. Whatever their differences, all the little bluebeards claimed vociferously, and indeed with some justice, that their mandate derived directly from him.

Nevertheless, as Bluebeard's Way covered the planet, difficulties arose. His original impulse, like his genes, had become grossly diluted. There were accidents and there were heresies, there were mutations and there were mutants. And there were even times – this happened particularly in the heat of battle – when even respect for property somehow went missing, albeit only briefly. To list all the heresies, many of them ill-considered and ill-thought out, e.g. 'The acquisition of property is not the true end of man,' would take too long; but there are two, which despite their illogic deserve special mention. The first of these was an incipient rumour: 'Everyone is Bluebeard'. Its very simplicity, or rather its simple-mindedness, proved an asset. No proof was offered; no rationale required. If pressed, the proponents might reply, "We are all descended from Bluebeard, therefore we are Bluebeard." It has created chaos. The second and more recent heresy was an offshoot of the first, and even more irrational. It stated that those who were property could nevertheless hold property themselves. Obviously this was nonsense, but when this was pointed out, the heretics declared that those who were property were no longer property. To put it crudely it liberated cows. To the end that we see: stray cows walking the streets, unkempt and unlooked after. Bleating calves. What self-respecting man will tend to property over which his claim is not apparent? And most hideous travesty of all: independent cows – what can the term mean? – with vestigial beards eking out a meagre living.

Yet even today a few faithful sons of Bluebeard remain, their genes undiluted, their minds unclouded, their message clear: BACK TO FUNDAMENTALS. Authority and Territory are the Rights of Man. Their programme is simple: females to be kept barefoot and pregnant; surplus males to be cleared off the land. It is possible that Bluebeard's Way might yet be restored to its primal purity.

Also by Suniti Namjoshi . . .

Feminist Fables
(new edition)

'There was once a man who thought he could do anything, even be a woman. So he acquired a baby, changed its diapers and fed the damn thing three times a night. He did all the housework, was deferential to men, and got worn out. But he had a brother, Jack Cleverfellow, who hired a wife, and got it all done.'

— The Tale of Two Brothers

Feminist Fables represents an ingenious reworking of fairy-tales, Greek and Sanskrit mythology, mixed with the author's original material and vivid imagination.

This book is an indispensable feminist classic.

Suniti Namjoshi was born in Bombay, India. She taught for some years at the University of Toronto, and now lives in England. Her books include *The Conversations of Cow*, *The Blue Donkey Fables* and *The Mothers of Maya Diip*.

Sybil:
The Glide of Her Tongue
Gillian Hanscombe

'Gillian Hanscombe performs a feat of lesbian imagination in this stunning sequence. Her sybilic voice, familiar and strange at once, radiates both vision and anger in a prose that echoes the music of our thoughts back to us. *Sybil* gives us a lesbian erotic, a lesbian politics, a lesbian tradition, grounded in what Suniti Namjoshi defines as the prophetic. Welcome to lesbian imagination singing at full range.'

– Daphne Marlatt

'That *Sybil* happily bears comparison with the works of Sappho, Virginia Woolf and Adrienne Rich is, in my view, a measure of just how important this work is to lesbian literature, and therefore to literature in general.'

– Suniti Namjoshi

'*Sybil: The Glide of Her Tongue* is a prophetic fugue in lesbian past, present and future time, Sybilline tidings of lesbian existence.'

– Mary Meigs

'O I am enamoured of *Sybil*. Gillian Hanscombe is one of the most insightfully ironic, deliciously lyrical voices we have writing amongst us today.'

– Betsy Warland

'A book where the lesbian voice meditates the essential vitality of she-dykes who have visions. A book where Gillian Hanscombe's poetry opens up meaning in such a way that it provides for beauty and awareness, for a space where one says yes to a lesbian we of awareness.'

– Nicole Brossard

'*Sybil* is an exciting and compelling work. It is hard to think of any poet in Australia who can equal Hanscombe's virtuosity and power.'

– Bev Roberts, *Australian Book Review*

Perverse Serenity
Robyn Rowland

What happens when an Australian feminist falls in love with an Irish monk?

'Here is a picture of a woman's divided loves, for a love in Ireland and for one in Australia, drawn with rare honesty and a compelling strength of observation which involves the reader.

Here is writing not afraid to be vulnerable, not trapped in literary artifice, not reticent about emotion, its hopes, its tears, its withdrawals and assertions, which we all share and which enrich our humanity.

A memorable picture emerges of a contemporary woman, intelligent and able to feel deeply, who is not afraid to feel the incompleteness, the unfinished edges of human love.'

– Barrett Reid

A leading critic of reproductive technologies, Robyn Rowland is also a poet. Reviewers described her first book, *Filigree in Blood*, as 'powerful and commanding', 'with that degree of integrity which makes one pay attention'.

Poems from the Madhouse
Sandy Jeffs

and

Now Millennium
Deborah Staines

The language challenges her with fifty names for madness, writing of a life of vigilance and struggle, she enlarges our understanding of human capacity. These repeated acts of courage, Sandy Jeffs' poems, "toil to make a harmony of disorder".

– Judith Rodriguez

This is disturbing but quite wonderful poetry, because of its clarity, its humour, its imagery, and the insights it gives us into being human, being mad, being sane. I read and read – and was profoundly moved. I delighted in it as poetry; I was touched by its honesty, courage and vulnerability.

– Anne Deveson

Deborah Staines' respect for and awareness of language's dynamic possibilities bring inner and outer worlds attentively alive.

– Fay Zwicky

This book is really wild . . . There's so much passion and commitment there and she's drunk with words.

– Dorothy Hewett